I'M GONNA PUSH THROUGH!

atheneum

ATHENEUM BOOKS FOR YOUNG READERS

An imprint of Simon & Schuster Children's Publishing Division

1230 Avenue of the Americas, New York, New York 10020

Text copyright © 2020 by Jasmyn Wright

Illustrations copyright © 2020 by Shannon Wright

ATHENEUM BOOKS FOR YOUNG READERS is a registered trademark of Simon & Schuster, Inc.
Atheneum logo is a trademark of Simon & Schuster, Inc. For information about special discounts for bulk
purchases, please contact Simon & Schuster Special Sales at 1-866-506-1949 or business@simonandschuster.com.

The Simon & Schuster Speakers Bureau can bring authors to your live event.
For more information or to book an event, contact the Simon & Schuster Speakers Bureau at 1-866-248-3049
or visit our website at www.simonspeakers.com.

Book design by Greg Stadnyk

The text for this book was set in Kirkby and Leftover Crayon.

The illustrations for this book were rendered digitally.

Manufactured in China

1119 SCP

First Edition

2 4 6 8 10 9 7 5 3 1

CIP data for this book is available from the Library of Congress.

ISBN 978-1-5344-3965-8

ISBN 978-1-5344-3966-5 (eBook)

To God, who is my ultimate source and strength. To my mom and grandmom, who nurture the creativity of my gifts. To my dad and older brother, whose personalities and humor help me push through. To my younger, autistic brother Julian, whose energy and spirit light up ANY space. To all of my students, who helped bring this message to life. To anybody in the world struggling to see their strength because it's clouded by the barrier of doubt, just know that you too can Push Through!
—J. W.

For Riverview Elementary School and
Broad Rock Elementary School
—S. W.

I'M GONNA PUSH THROUGH!

JASMYN WRIGHT

ART BY SHANNON WRIGHT

Atheneum Books for Young Readers

NEW YORK LONDON TORONTO SYDNEY NEW DELHI

Hold your head high.
No matter what stands in the way
of your dreams, remember this:

YOU can push through anything!

If someone tells you it's too hard, don't you *ever* listen.
You tell them,

I'm gonna push through!

Think of those before you who never gave up:

Barack Obama . . .
He pushed through!

Malala Yousafzai . . .
She pushed through!

Oprah Winfrey . . .
She pushed through!

George Takei . . .
He pushed through!

Jillian Mercado . . .
She pushed through!

Diane Guerrero . . .
She pushed through!

LaDonna Brave Bull Allard . . .
She pushed through!

Jamie Brewer . . .
She pushed through!

Marley Dias . . .
She pushed through!

LeBron James . . .
He pushed through!

Stephen Hawking . . .
He pushed through!

Sharice Davids . . .
She pushed through!

Juan Felipe Herrera . . .
He pushed through!

Mirai Nagasu . . .
She pushed through!

Tyler Perry . . .
He pushed through!

Trevor Noah . . .
He pushed through!

And if *they* can do it, you can do it too.

You say it now.

If they can do it, I can do it too!

What if it's too hard?

I'm gonna
push through!

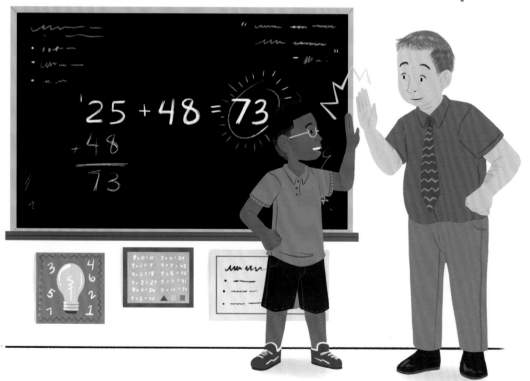

What if it's too tough?

I'm gonna push through!

What if it's too rough?

I'm gonna push through!

What if you don't know how to do it?

I'm gonna push through!

What if you just *can't* do it?

I'm gonna push through!

What if you're just too young?

That's not true!

What if you're not good enough?

That's not true!

Tell me why . . .

I can do ANYTHING I put my mind to!

I believe in you.

Chin up!

Believe in yourself.

Head high!

Turn and tell someone,
encourage them and say:

I believe in you!

Now ask them:

Do you believe in yourself?

Point to yourself and say:

I believe in me. I WILL believe in myself!

Remember, you were born for a . . .

REASON!

Your life has . . .

MEANING!

You were birthed with a . . .

PURPOSE!

And it will be your goal to . . .

FIND IT!

Because one day
in this world you will . . .

MAKE A DIFFERENCE!

Shirley Chisholm

Katherine Johnson

Sarla Thakral

Audrey Hepburn

Serena Williams

Martin Luther King Jr.

And use your
footprint to . . .

LEAVE AN
IMPRINT!

Marlee Matlin

Anna May Wong

Muhammad Ali

Cesar Chavez

Marsha P. Johnson

Anne Frank

Russell Means

Stevie Wonder

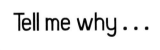
Tell me why . . .

Sylvia Mendez

Sally Ride

The Tuskegee Airmen

Bruce Lee

Marie Tharp

Maria Tallchief

I can push through ANYTHING I put my mind to!

Excellent.

Now don't let anyone in the world
tell you otherwise.

A Note from the Author

If a bird never knew that it had wings, how could it know that it could fly? That's what the Push Through movement is about. It's about exposure to self, and the hidden power and tools we all have inside of us to keep going. It's about convincing people that they are ENOUGH, and that they are born equipped with a unique set of talents and skills that will help them maximize their potential and overcome life's inevitable adversities. Push Through aims to empower and inspire individuals to be the best version of themselves by tapping into their inner strengths. As a teacher, this is the mind-set that I instill in my students. I know that if I can reach them at their core to build their emotional resiliency, accountability, and self-awareness, I can succeed in making them true life-long learners.

I began my teaching journey in 2010. I've taught in low-income and inner-city communities, and I knew that my students needed more than the bare minimum to help them excel. Many were from broken families, some of them were even homeless, and a lot of them have experienced realities that many adults couldn't even fathom. Coupled with their daily adversities, a great majority of my children struggled academically, had anger issues, and needed proper coping strategies.

I'm determined that by the time my children leave my class at the end of each year, they are going to LOVE and believe in themselves! I make it my mission to help them shift their perspectives on challenging situations and prove that the barrier they once considered an unwavering mountain is really only a flickable pebble. The goal is to help them to excel even when they aren't under the supervision of their parents, myself, or any other adult that loves and cares for them. I want to teach them strategies that they can use to PUSH themselves to not only find their wings, but to flap them and soar.

Through teaching children the concept of emotional resilience, educators and parents have the power to transform "I can't" to "I can" and "I'm not good enough" to "I'm born with a gift." We can teach this mind-set by setting and enforcing high expectations, emphasizing accountability and self-awareness, and helping children believe that they can not only achieve these qualities, but that they are WORTHY of achieving them.

When I started teaching third grade in Philadelphia, the curriculum was really challenging. Instead of accepting the challenge and looking at it as a way to grow and become stronger, my children uttered negative affirmations and excuses such as, "There are too many words in this text to read!" or "Man, I can't do this!" My children were predominantly

African American. They didn't know about their wings, nor did they believe that they could fly. I told my children every day that they have a purpose in this world, and they mustn't give up on themselves, because there are people who are waiting on their gifts. On the back wall of my classroom, I plastered the question, "What Will You Do to Make a Difference in the World?" Underneath were pictures of heroic African Americans who've overcome adversity and left their imprint on the world. I wanted the children to know that there are people like them—who grew up and experienced the same hardships, and who look like them—who have also overcome adversity. I hoped they could see that they weren't too young to make a difference. That there are influential African Americans who've beat the odds, didn't give up during hard times, and as a result, changed the world.

I'd reference these heroes throughout daily lessons, using their journeys as examples of resiliency. Whenever I said the word "resilient" in class, my children asked me what it meant. Eventually, I substituted the words "Push Through," which became our class motto. I wanted them to know that their past doesn't define them, their present doesn't have to hinder them, and their future is waiting on them.

The actual words and hand movements of the original Push Through mantra came to me one evening as I was getting ready for work the next day. I started hearing a mix of questions and phrases in my head. The words were so strong and fluent. I sat and wrote

them all down. I began thinking about all of the conversations we'd had in class about pushing through, and I worked those into the mantra. I even included some prominent historical influencers. When I took this affirmation to my children the following day, they fell in LOVE with it!

It became our daily affirmation, and we recited it every morning before class. Push Through was our classroom culture, and children used it to encourage one another, themselves, and even me as their teacher! It shifted the way they spoke about themselves and to one another. They'd say phrases like, "Ms. Wright, this test is challenging, but I'm going to push through anyway and try my best!" Not only were they taking accountability and eliminating excuses, but they were also figuring out their own strategies to excel in class! Push Through even managed classroom behavior. If a child was off-task and not abiding by my behavioral expectations, other children would say to him or her, "C'mon, push through! I believe you can fix the problem. Focus!"

One morning in November 2016, I decided to record the mantra. A student said to me, "Ms. Wright, you should put this on your Facebook page so that your mom can see it!" To my surprise, within twenty-four hours, the Facebook post reached 150,000 views. In one week, our video reached 3.7 million views. Once our video went viral, it strengthened the culture of our classroom. I vividly remember one child coming up to me and saying, "You were right! We aren't too young to make a difference in the world! Our voices really are powerful!" The mantra encouraged my children to be brave and courageous by pushing through mental barriers and to solve problems despite ambiguity.

In 2017, Gap Kids featured our class and mantra as a part of their back-to-school campaign. The campaign consisted of a thirty-second commercial and mini-documentary based on a shortened version of our original classroom mantra.

What initially started as a lesson for my inner-city third-graders has spread to become a global empowerment initiative that's inspiring people of all ages. The Push Through movement is present in classrooms and communities in more than twenty-three countries so far, and has been translated into multiple languages. It's been used in K–12 settings and professional work settings, as well as college classrooms. It's received worldwide media coverage and is changing lives around the globe. Push Through empowers children to be their best!

The popularity of the mantra inspired me to create a nonprofit: the Push Through Organization. The organization is a movement with international footprints that aims to empower and inspire people of all ages to overcome any adversity. We offer teacher-training programs, curriculum, consulting, partnerships, and motivational workshops.

When we show people that they were born with a talent that sets them apart, we help them see that they have a purpose for existing. Once they see and believe that they have a purpose, they understand that they must put in work in order to reach their goal. They have to shift their way of thinking from a fixed mind-set to a growth mind-set. They aren't defeated by mistakes. Their environment doesn't limit them. Challenges don't scare them. Instead, they are empowered and inspired to find and exert their gifts and use them. Once students learn how to access their untapped potential, they can Push Through and believe that they can conquer ANYTHING that they put their minds to!

—Jasmyn Wright, M.Ed

To get involved and/or find out more about the Push Through Organization, the cities and countries where we are present, and what we are up to next, please visit our website: wepushthrough.org.

Barack Obama is a Nobel Peace Prize winner and a former President of the United States of America. He pushed through racial tension and stereotypes to become the first African American to be elected president.

Malala Yousafzai is a Pakistani activist and the youngest person to win the Nobel Prize. Best known for her bravery against the Taliban and her advocacy for the education of women and children, her passion has spread to become a global movement.

Oprah Winfrey is an African American multi-billionaire who overcame extreme poverty and repeated sexual abuse during her childhood years. One of the most powerful and influential women in the world, Winfrey is best known for being a successful talk-show host, entrepreneur, philanthropist, and social influencer.

George Takei is a Japanese American activist, actor, and writer best known for his role on *Star Trek*. During World War II, he and his family experienced hardship and racial discrimination when they were forced to live in a Japanese American internment camp. Takei is a political activist championing a number of human rights issues, especially LGBTQ rights and social justice for immigrants.

Jillian Mercado is a Dominican American fashion model born with muscular dystrophy. Mercado uses a wheelchair, so she pushed through barriers in the industry to become one of the few professional models with a physical disability.

Diane Guerrero is a Colombian American actress, author, and feminist, who advocates for immigration reform. When she was fourteen, her parents were deported and sent back to Colombia.

LaDonna Brave Bull Allard, a Native American activist and historian, is a member of the Standing Rock Sioux Tribe. Known for founding the Sacred Stone Camp, Allard led one of the largest resistance protests against the Dakota Access Pipeline.

Jamie Brewer is an American actress, and the first model with Down syndrome to walk the runway at New York Fashion week. Brewer is also an activist who speaks up for the rights of others born with Down syndrome.

Marley Dias is a Caribbean American activist and author who noticed that the books she was reading in school didn't have main characters that looked like her. To solve this problem, Dias launched a campaign and movement called #1000BlackGirlBooks at the age of eleven.

LeBron James is an African American professional basketball player considered one of the greatest in the world. The son of a single-parent mother and an incarcerated father, James pushed through a childhood in poverty and unstable living environments and opened the I Promise School to help at-risk children in his hometown of Akron, Ohio.

Stephen Hawking was diagnosed with a progressive neurodegenerative disease called ALS in his early twenties, and was almost completely paralyzed. However, none of that stopped Hawking from becoming a best-selling author and one of the world's leading physicists.

Sharice Davids is an LGBT Native American attorney, entrepreneur, mixed-martial arts professional, and politician. She was raised by a single mother, who served in the military. A member of the Ho-Chunk Nation, Davids made history as one of the first Native Americans to serve in the United States Congress. She was elected in November 2018 as the Democratic representative for Kansas's 3rd Congressional District.

Juan Felipe Herrera is a Mexican American poet, author, teacher, and activist. The son of migrant farmers, Herrera moved a lot as a child, living in tents and trailers. He taught himself to read and write English, and he used the personal accounts of his childhood experiences to create and publish more than twenty books. He was the first Latino to be named a United States Poet Laureate.

Mirai Nagasu is a Japanese American professional figure skater who pushed toward her goal of being in the Olympics. Nagasu was once rejected from the USA Team, but used that to encourage herself to learn from her mistakes and work harder. In 2018, Nagasu was the first American woman to land a triple axel jump in competition, which helped place Team USA in third place during the Olympics.

Tyler Perry is an African American producer, director, writer, and filmmaker who persisted through adversities in his youth, including homelessness, molestation, physical abuse from his father, and even attempted suicide. Perry decided to pursue a career in playwriting, but his first play was a failure. Choosing to push through and not give up on his dream, Perry is now one of the most famous and successful filmmakers in the world.

Trevor Noah is a South African comedian, Emmy-winning talk-show host, political commentator, and producer. As the child of a black mother and a white father, Noah was considered "illegal" by the country's apartheid government and faced violence and hostility during his younger years. He used that adversity to fuel and excel in his gift in comedy.